Chief Stephen's Parky

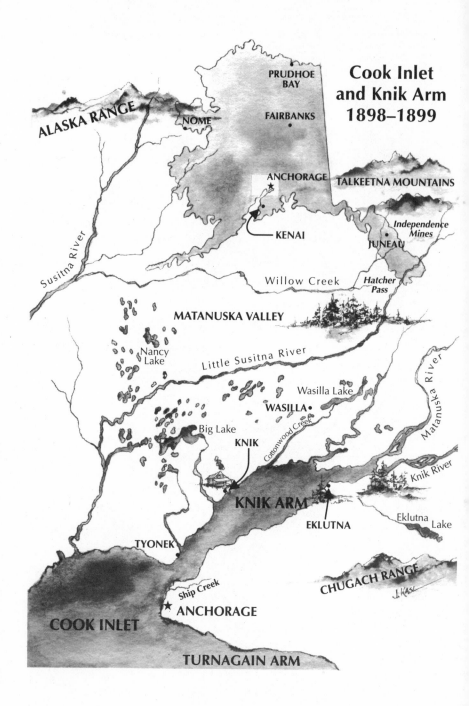

Cook Inlet and Knik Arm 1898–1899

ALASKA RANGE

PRUDHOE BAY

NOME

FAIRBANKS

ANCHORAGE

TALKEETNA MOUNTAINS

KENAI

Susitna River

Independence Mines

JUNEAU

Willow Creek

Hatcher Pass

MATANUSKA VALLEY

Nancy Lake

Little Susitna River

Matanuska River

Wasilla Lake

WASILLA

Big Lake

KNIK

Cottonwood Creek

Knik River

KNIK ARM

Knik River

EKLUTNA

Eklutna Lake

TYONEK

CHUGACH RANGE

J. Kast

Ship Creek

ANCHORAGE

COOK INLET

TURNAGAIN ARM

Chief Stephen's Parky

One Year in the Life of an Athapascan Girl

◆◆◆

Ann Chandonnet

Illustrations
by Janette Kasl

ROBERTS RINEHART PUBLISHERS
IN COOPERATION WITH
THE COUNCIL FOR INDIAN EDUCATION

Copyright © 1989, 1993 by Ann Chandonnet

International Standard Book Number 1-879373-39-4
Library of Congress Catalog Card Number 92-061910

Library of Congress Cataloging in Publication Data

Chandonnet, Ann.
    Chief Stephen's parky: one year in the life of an Athapascan girl
/ by Ann Chandonnet ; illustrations by Janette Kasl.
        p.   cm.
    Summary: As the young wife of a Tanaina, or Dena'ina, Indian chief
spends a year making a special parka for her husband, she reveals
the lives of her people in Alaska at the end of the nineteenth
century.
    ISBN 1-879373-39-4
    [1. Dena'ina Indians—Juvenile fiction. 2. Dena'ina Indians-
-Fiction. 3. Dena'ina Indians—Women—Fiction. 4. Indians of North
America—Alaska—Fiction.] I. Kasl, Janette, ill. II. Title.
PZ7.C359654Ch   1993   92-61910
[Fic]—dc20   CIP
                                                             AC

Published in the United States by
Roberts Rinehart Publishers, Post Office Box 666
Niwot, Colorado 80544

Published in Canada by
Key·Porter Books, 70 The Esplanade
Toronto, Ontario M5E 1R2

Published in Ireland by
Roberts Rinehart
3 Bayview Terrace
Schull, West Cork

Contents

To my sons, Yves and Alexandre; to Cynthia, Maxim,
and Sam; and to the children of Knik, Wasilla,
Eklutna, Palmer, Anchorage, Tyonek, and Kenai.
Long may you pick berries and cut fish.

Acknowledgements

A book like *Chief Stephen's Parky* could never have been
written without the groundwork in Athapascan culture laid
by ethnologists like Cornelius Osgood and Frederica deLa-
guna; by linguists like James Kari, James Fall, and Priscilla
Kari; and by native informants like Shem Pete, Peter Kali-
fornsky, and the late Mike Alex. I owe a debt to them all, and
to many others like them not named here. I am also grateful
to archaeologists William and Karen Workman of the University of Alaska, Anchorage, for always answering my ques-
tions with unsparing courtesy. My husband also merits
thanks for his patience with this project. And to the late poet-
laureate Margaret Mielke, who suggested in 1976 that I inter-
view Mike Alex.

The Council for Indian Education Series

The Council for Indian Education is a non-profit organization devoted to teacher training and to the publication of materials to aid in Indian education. All books are selected by an Indian editorial board and are approved for use with Indian children. Proceeds are used for the publication of more books for Indian children. Roberts Rinehart Publishers copublishes select manuscripts to aid the Council for Indian Education in the distribution of these books to wider markets, to aid in their production, and to support the Council's educational programs.

Introduction

The story of *Chief Stephen's Parky* is the fictional story of a typical Tanaina (or Dena'ina) Athapascan village on Cook Inlet, northwest of the modern city of Anchorage, Alaska.

The Tanaina Indians are one of the Athapascan peoples, a widely-distributed Native American linguistic group. They are related linguistically to Indians in California, Oregon, and Canada, as well as to the Navaho and Apache of the American Southwest.

Early ancestors of modern Athapascans may have crossed the land bridge (Beringia) from Asia to North America 30,000 years ago. The term Athapascan (also spelled Athabascan) is an Algonkian word used by the Cree to refer to the "strangers of the North" who lived around Lake Athabaska in Canada.

However, other linguistic evidence says Athapasca is a Cree word meaning "where there are reeds," and Athapascan is therefore translated as "people of the grass/reeds."

Lake Athabasca lies astride the Alberta-Saskatchewan border. The lake is 208 miles long and 32 miles wide, or about forty percent the size of Lake Ontario. It was unknown to caucasians until 1771.

Data is inconclusive about where Athapascan culture originated. One theory supposes it originated in Canada, and gradually spread into the interior of Alaska. Archeological evidence is clear that by 500 AD Athapascans occupied interior Alaska, the terrain known as taiga.

The Tanaina came to the shores of Cook Inlet at least 600 years ago, and perhaps as long as 9,000 years ago. The Tanaina numbered about 5,000 when white men first came to the area in the late 1700s. Today there are only 1,000 Tanaina, of whom only about 150 speak the language. The Tanaina

traditionally inhabited an area of about 41,000 square miles—
about the size of the state of Ohio. This territory extended all
around Cook Inlet and inland to Lake Clark and Lake Ili-
amna, as well as to the upper Mulchatna and Stony Rivers.
Like other Athapascans, the Tanaina were hunter-gatherers.
In their year-round quest for food and natural resources, they
developed an extensive system of trails over which they traveled, making use of various fish, fowl, and animals in different habitats at appropriate seasons.

The Athapascans are a clever, inventive people who knew
how to make do with what was at hand. They were marvelous
walkers and often traveled fearlessly across glaciers and over
mountains to meet people and explore new lands on the other
side. On Cook Inlet and its tributary rivers they used skin
boats and Eskimo-style kayaks.

Chief Stephen's Parky describes the migratory seasonal cycle
typical of the Tanaina, and also shows them at a point in their
history when modern technology and European ways were
beginning to change their traditional way of life forever. The
story was inspired by a photograph of Chief Stephen in a
ground squirrel parky. Stephen was born *Qatsen*, a member
of the *Nulchina* clan. The photograph was taken about 1907
by Orville Herning, a prospector, storekeeper and amateur
photographer who lived in Knik and later in neighboring
Wasilla from 1898 to 1947. Stephen, or Big Stephen, worked
for Herning, and Herning mentions him off and on in his
diary. Other Herning photos were used as the basis for some
of the pen and ink illustrations by artist Janette Kasl.

Knik village was typical of an Athapascan village in 1898.
Photo by Orville Herning, collection of the author.

The Tanaina Months
(after Cornelius Osgood and James Fall)

Month	Meaning	Tanaina
January	"little snow melts"	*Soknoykna*
February	"when sun makes a little water"	*Winondoniyasi*
March	"birds come back"	*No.t'aq'e.no*
April	"geese month"	*Nut'aq'i n'u*
	"half the candlefish (hooligan) let loose"	*Nondanq'ene.si*
May	"egg month"	*Qagoyano*
June	"king salmon run"	*Liqagaano*
	"king salmon month"	*Liq'aka'a n'u*
July	"birds moulting"	*Kanedaqueno*
August	"half yellow leaves"	*Wonxdiciqi*
September	"half winter"	*Wonqesani*
October	"sun on horizon"	*Minondaqeosi*
November	"visitors"	*Qatggentdalna*
	"snow falls"	*Minonhosi*
December	"not very cold"	*Minondicinasi*

Chapter One

Olga Plans a Parky

Shortly before the first snowfall of September 1898, Chief Stephen's young wife, Olga, went out to collect alder bark.

Her toes felt the ground growing cold through her moose hide moccasin soles. "Soon winter will be here," she thought to herself.

Olga was preparing to make her husband a new parky, or winter overjacket. The alder bark would be used for dye. She was happy every time she thought about her plan to make him a special jacket with fancy trim. But she was also anxious. Could she make one worthy of such a handsome chief and clever leader?

It would take nearly a year to gather all the materials necessary for the new parky. But Olga was determined to make it the best one she had ever sewn.

As she pushed her way into one of the dense thickets that surrounded her small village, Knik, she was careful not to tear her dress or scratch her hands on the prickly wild roses and thorny Devil's Club. She paused in a warm patch of sunlight that filtered through the tree-tops. She nibbled on some high bush cranberries that grew as tall as her nose. Then she stepped into a narrow moose trail through the trees. The dark spruce and bushes grew so close together that it was hard for her to squeeze through. In a few moments she reached a grove of alders. They were beautiful trees, fifteen feet high, with many trunks curving out from the root, like the

1

fingers from the palm of my hand, she thought. Some alders had trunks five inches across, their bark dotted white with the spots of great age, like the dappling of a caribou fawn, thought Olga.

Olga chose a large alder trunk that bent up from the damp leaf litter toward the golden fall sun. A portion of the trunk curved out at elbow height. As a young girl, Olga might have pulled herself up to sit and dream on such a convenient perch. Now she was a wife with work to do, and this broad trunk, where it bent parallel to the ground, formed a handy table top.

She began to scrape off and peel back the thin gray outer bark of the trunk. Taking a curved horn paddle from her skirt pocket, she scraped away the reddish inner bark in very fine particles. These crumbs she caught in a small pouch made of seal intestine. The crumbly red bits would be dye—rubbed directly on the skin she would use for the parky's trim.

As she scraped, Olga could picture her husband following caribou for many miles in deep snow, or climbing the steep trail to the twin peaks above Eklutna Lake. Between the peaks was a mineral lick where mountain sheep gathered. Stephen would need a warm parky for such difficult hunting trips.

Now eighteen years old, Olga had married Chief Stephen three years ago. Their baby son, Michael, nicknamed Mishka, was now eighteen months old.

Olga and other Athapascan girls learned adult skills early in life. Olga was already respected by other talented Knik seamstresses for her talent with sinew, hide and dyes made from wild plants and bark. She had proved her cleverness by decorating the skin garments she made with bits of contrasting fur or scraps of bright felt or cloth from Knik Station, the Alaska Commercial Company store across Cook Inlet from her village.

This garment would be even more beautiful. This time she would use trade beads, caribou hooves, and shells that would show what a good hunter Stephen was. Perhaps she would even stitch on a row of puffin beaks which would clack together like a choir of small bells.

Olga paid close attention to her task. When she had enough of the red bark in her pouch, she returned to her log cabin home. There she pulled from her sewing kit some sealskin she had tanned during the short summer, when the weather was fine enough to soak skins outdoors. She had soaked the seal skins for two days to loosen the coarse hair. When the hair was loose, she had scraped it away with a tool made of caribou antler. Then she rinsed the hairless skins well in fresh water. Finally they were laced to a frame of willow to dry.

Olga continued the long tanning process by rubbing seal brains into the skins. Others were soaked in urine. Athapascans and Eskimos used every ingredient that came to hand. Olga wasted nothing.

When the skins had soaked sufficiently, she kneaded and worked them for hours to make them soft and pliable. If skins were not handled and rubbed, they would be stiff and uncomfortable to wear. A man who had poorly tanned, ill-fitting clothing was a man whose wife was lazy—or a man who had no wife. Olga took pride in every item she made for Stephen, and when his clothes were wet or torn, she carefully dried or mended them.

For her special project, Olga experimented. To dye her sealskin a powerfully deep red, she mixed her powdered alder bark with a little water. Then she pounded it into a paste in an old alderwood bowl. She rubbed the paste on the prepared sealskin and allowed it to dry. When she brushed the residue away, the sealskin had not taken the color as well as wolverine would have, so she repeated the process. When the skin satisfied her, she stored it away. She would cut it into pretty, red bands to decorate the hem of her husband's parky.

John, Olga's nine-year-old brother, carved a spoon from mountain goat horn as he watched his sister hard at work. This was his fourth spoon, and he was trying to sculpt a mountain goat's face on the broad end of the handle. He had learned to carve by silently watching the men of Knik for hours as they carved. "Will you sew me a new parky, too, Olga?" he asked.

"First I must sew one for your Uncle Stephen," she answered, teasing him a little. "You know, John, that the hunters of the village must be warm when they look for white hares against the white snow, when they trap marten and follow the hoofprints of moose. Hunters must have the best parkies and boots and socks. . . ."

Olga stopped suddenly, and smiled. "You are growing so fast, John, that I can see your ankles between your moccasins and your trousers. In fact, I can see nearly to your knees. And you bring in many grouse for the stew pot. You, too, must have a new parky—and some new trousers!"

John was pleased. He smiled, too. But he said nothing, and inspected the pointed, listening ears of his carved goat very closely.

When Olga finished dyeing her sealskin, she turned to other chores. There was much to do before winter came. There were tart, red, lowbush cranberries to pick in the forest clearings. The cranberries would be stored in barrels of cold water. Their waxy skins kept them fresh for many months.

The trailing evergreen vines of the cranberry followed

the trunks of dead birch logs, which littered the forest floor. As she picked cranberries, Olga recalled the years when she and other Knik children enjoyed lying on their stomachs on these soft mounds of decaying wood, moss, and vines as they lazily picked berries into birchbark buckets. Their mothers would scold, trying to hurry them along, because soon the frosts would come, darkening the berries, and they would fall into the moss and be lost as food for the village.

Now Olga hurried, for she knew that in Alaska winter would last for six long, cold months. Once the snow fell, it would not melt until spring. It would pile up and up, deeper and deeper, until there were several feet of it around the houses. Some winters there would be deep paths leading to the woodpile and the caches. There would be weeks and weeks when the temperature was below zero. Outdoors, it would hurt to breathe and the cold seemed to squeeze your skull between frosty hands. Fingertips dried, split, and began to bleed. Moccasins and mukluks squeaked on the dry, glittering snow packed in the yards of the village.

Olga remembered a winter when snow that reached the belly of John's dog, Sodaa, fell in one night. In the morning, her father was unable to find the dogs' houses, although they were raised on two-foot stilts. The tough, wiry dogs were snow bound and they slept patiently, their fluffy tails curled around to warm their noses, until her father finally dug them out.

Chapter Two

Winter in Knik Village

Olga was right to hurry to finish her skin curing and berry picking.

The very next day there was a frost, and the raspberries, rose hips, and cranberries began to darken on their canes, bushes, and vines. Brash ice crystals began to gather along the edges of the creeks and lakes. Cook Inlet took on a grayer color, and the waves that lapped against the sloping beach at Knik seemed slower, thicker, more sluggish. There were other signs, too. In big loops and swirls over the marshes, the mallards and Canada geese strengthened their wings and trained this summer's young ones for the long flight south.

Soon there was frost every day. Grasses began to lie flat. The tall fireweed, its magenta blossoms gone, and its parachuted seeds blown away, looked limp and ill. Birch and cottonwood leaves were dull brown, drooping—then falling and crunching underfoot as Olga scurried about her chores.

One morning there was an inch of snow outside Olga's cabin door. Winter had come to Knik.

Despite the snow and cold, Olga's brother John looked forward to the season of winter, because the children had many special games to enjoy. One was sliding. As soon as the lakes were frozen, they slid on the ice on old caribou pelts. Mothers scolded, because these pelts were the children's mattresses and blankets, but the children enjoyed sneaking them out of the cabins and sliding on them anyway.

When the snow deepened, the children played a game like soccer. They used a large ball sewn from caribou skin and stuffed with springy caribou hair. They loved to play with their ball late at night, by the light of the moon. On clear nights, when the moon was full, the stars seemed very close. The snow seemed to glow with a light of its own, and the tall Chugach mountains across Knik Arm glowed, too. Sometimes the Northern Lights would dance and sing to them in waves of yellow, pink and green.

John had a small sled, to which he hitched his two dogs, Kanaa and Sodaa. Sometimes his friends Simeon and Theodore broke trail for the dogs. The boys plowed on ahead in the fresh snow, wearing snowshoes over their mukluks. They took turns being the lead, because it was very tiring to make a path through the snow in a new direction. Although they wore long parkas that went down to their knees and deep hoods that protected their ears and cheeks, their noses were red when they returned and the dogs were hungry for their meal of dried fish.

When it was too cold to play outside, John, Simeon, and Theodore liked to play guessing games. One would tell a riddle about something he had seen in the forest, or had heard about from the elders. Everyone else would have to guess from the clues given what that something was. Whoever guessed correctly received a prize, usually a bit of food. Some of the riddles had been used year after year, like nursery rhymes. It was a challenge to make new riddles, but the adults often created new ones to test the children.

One evening that winter in 1898, Olga asked the boys this riddle:

When I wake up in the morning
I am thin and bad tempered.
I eat all day,
While everyone keeps out of my way.
In the evening, I am fat and go to bed content.
I pull the furs over my head so no one sees me.
Who am I?

"You were an old grump this morning when you crawled out of your skins," Simeon mumbled to John. But he knew this wasn't the answer; he just said this to distract the other boys and give himself more time to think.

The boys thought hard, wrinkling their brows and pursing their lips as they concentrated. They knew Olga was making biscuits, and they all wanted one.

"You're a brown bear!" John burst out excitedly. "You hibernate all winter. When you come out of your den in the spring, you are hungry and grumpy. When you eat all summer, you get fat, and go into your den again. You dig into a hill so no one sees you."

"Good, John," said Olga, passing biscuits to all.

Many of the adults remembered riddles from their own childhoods. They challenged the children with this one:

I sleep on my back in a wet cradle.
I cannot walk.
I open the door to my food with a rock.
Who am I?

The children almost laughed aloud because this riddle was so easy. They all shouted out, "Sea otter!"

"He cracks open the shells of clams while floating on his back in the ocean. He holds a rock on his chest and smashes the clams against it," said Alex, as if reciting a lesson he had memorized. He could almost feel his fingers stroking a silky sea otter pelt as he said this.

Then came a more difficult riddle:

My head is light in the time of new leaves
And heavy when the leaves are falling.
Under my chin
I wear an empty sewing kit
That swings and swings.
It looks like a church bell yet it doesn't sing.
My four legs are like the stilts
Of a food storage cache.
Who am I?

"It's a bull moose, who loses his heavy antlers and grows another rack every year," Alex said quickly. "He has a beardthing under his chin."

Matrona recited the next riddle:

I turn my back on my enemies.
I cannot shoot my arrows,
But they work in deep.
Sometimes they kill.
I chew bark and twigs, but I smile
When I chew tools from the woodpile.
Who am I?

"A porcupine," all the children said at once.

"He likes the salt on axe handles, the salt left by human skin," said John, his face clouding a little as he remembered now that Matrona had recently scolded him for leaving tools where animals could get to them and gnaw on them.

Cheeda, Stephen's wise old mother, remembered riddles, too:

My feathery snowshoes
Need no knotted bindings of babiche
At the ankles.
I walk on fresh, soft drifts without falling in.
I change color to match the ground,
Now white, now brown.
Round and round
In circles I march,
Before I take to the air.
What am I?

"I know, I know," Simeon said, eagerly. "It's a ptarmigan. I hunt them. I eat them. Mother uses ptarmigan feathers to stuff our pillows."
Now Gronia, Olga's sister, told her favorite riddle:

I can barely walk
Because my feet are so close to my tail.
I build my nest close to the shore,
So I can scoot right into the lake.

I have many songs, some sad, some glad.
I dance on water with my mate
And watch my child closely
While he learns to fish without bait.
When eagle comes looking for prey,
Gull, fisher, and I chase him away.

"It's the loon," said Simeon, who loved to hunt birds, watch birds, and carve birds from chunks of soft, thick cottonwood bark. Simeon dreamed of being a bald eagle and spying on Knik from strong, ten-foot wings. If he were an eagle, he would swoop down on John and Alex and his little baby sister Inga and startle them, make the dogs bark and leap, and then he would perch in the tallest spruce near his cabin and watch his mother heating rocks in the fire to cook dinner, and stirring her salmon stew.

But because he knew Gronia loved the beautiful Pacific loons and their chicks, he tried not to dream of how eagles eat young mallard ducklings and loon chicks. He thought of how the loon guards her baby, and how the other shore birds, who are usually enemies, gather to chase off eagles when they come circling the shore, looking for baby birds to eat.

The chores of gathering and splitting wood, melting clean snow for drinking and for cooking water, feeding and watering the dogs, checking snares and traplines took many hours each day. The children and adults did not have much time for amusements.

But one evening Chief Stephen told them a riddle that no one could solve:

> *I eat dirt*
> *And then when my stomach hurts*
> *I jump and shout,*
> *Shaking the ground about,*
> *And spit it out.*
> *Who am I?*

The children thought for a long time, but no one knew the answer. Finally, two days later, as she was putting away the bit of flint rock that her mother used to start fires, Caterina, Alex's eleven-year-old sister, realized what the answer must be.

"Volcano!" she shouted, out of breath after running to find the chief, who was covering his woodpile with spruce boughs to keep it dry. The chief smiled. He had once sailed many days in his Eskimo-style kayak to the southern part of Cook Inlet where mountains that smoked and sometimes shot out clouds of ash raised their rocky heads. When these volcanoes erupted, they spat out clouds of ash that made everything gray and dusty for hundreds of miles around. As Caterina's reward, he told her of that very voyage, and all the strange sights he had seen.

The children had time for riddles, but the young wife, Olga, had little. All the women were busy nearly every minute, especially now that the days were short and there was little light to work by.

The women kept their snare lines going throughout the winter. They trapped food for the dogs and for an occasional rabbit stew. They checked the snares every five days. Snowshoe hares were caught in almost the same way ground squirrels were, with sinew tied to a spring pole. Exploring the undergrowth looking for tender buds, the hare ran through the loop of sinew and the noose tightened around his neck while the pole lifted him into the air. A dog needed half a rabbit a day for food. The rabbit skins could be cut into strips and knitted into blankets or sewn into children's snow pants.

After the gathering and preparing of food and hot broth, one of the women's most important jobs was drying out wet clothing, especially mittens and fur socks. Clinging snow and ice were beaten off outdoors. The garments were hung near the fire and repeatedly turned inside out and then right side out again as they dried and then they were kneaded to keep them soft. An Alaskan with wet clothing will soon freeze to death. When grass

Mukluks are knee-high boots of skin and fur.

innersoles were damp and compressed, new ones must be made of dry grass gathered and stored during the summer.

Despite all her duties, Olga still found time to help the girls of fourteen and fifteen with their sewing and beadwork. Soon these girls would be wives and would need these skills. They began with easy projects like caribou

socks. Then they made men's knee high boots or mukluks. The boot soles were made of tough caribou skin or
moose hide. When the girls could sew expertly, they were
allowed to begin making parkys.

There were no chairs in the small village of Knik,
although some of the bigger families had stools around
their tables. Most of the girls sat flat on the floor, their
legs straight out before them as they cut and stitched.
The poor light from fireplaces and kerosene lanterns
made sewing hard on their eyes, but it had to be done.

All winter Olga was busy and happy, and there were
many good times. However, Cheeda and some of the
other village elders were worried. Every winter they worried that their supplies of berries, dried fish, jerked meat
and fish oil might run out before spring, that there
would be a starving time.

Soon came the end of the month that white men call
"December." The Athapascans call this month *Minon-
dicinasi*, meaning "not very cold." Now the shortest days
of the year were past. Cheeda was relieved, for each new
day was longer by a few minutes of precious, warming
light.

When this time of year arrived, Olga began to antic-
ipate all the delights of spring squirrel camp, and even
to think about the spring to come. Then Cheeda and the
60 villagers would have green leaves and fresh roots to
eat, and Cheeda could stop poking into barrels and
boxes and counting on her fingers.

But before those days arrived, there first came the
colder days of January and February to get through. The
people called January *Soknoykna*, or "Little water
melts." February was *Winondoniyasi*, or "Sun makes a
little water." On the coldest days, when the temperature
dropped to minus 20°F and the wind whistled around

their cabins, seeming to pierce the thickest sod roof, the villagers tried to stay inside as much as possible. When they had to go outside for wood or to gather snow to melt for drinking water, eddies of dry snow were scouring the frozen landscape. The eddies moved like spirits who could find no rest. The blown snow stung the peoples' chapped faces as if it were sand.

Winter was hard on animals as well as people. Chief Stephen took his dogs warm water to drink, and watched with concern as the dogs coming back hitched to sleds used their teeth and tongues to remove thorns of ice from between their tender toes. On the coldest days, he brought his best dogs inside and let them rest near the fire. Sometimes John's dogs, Sodaa and Kanaa, were allowed to sleep with him in his nest of caribou skins.

Chapter Three

Muskrat Camp at Red Shirt Lake

Olga's family spent only part of the year in their sod-roofed cabins at Knik on Cook Inlet. Their cabins here were roomy and solid, suitable for the coldest months, when they lived like bears in their dens. But as the days grew longer, the sun warmer, Chief Stephen moved his family to muskrat camp twenty-five miles northwest at Red Shirt Lake. It took two days to walk there, on an old trail that crossed several creeks on rough bridges. The bridges were made by throwing spruce logs across the water.

Although it was often 40°F below and colder at Red Shirt Lake in the middle of winter, by mid-March temperatures began to rise above freezing. There were many lakes here: Skeetna, Butterfly, Lynx, Traders, Duck, and tiny Twin Shirt Lakes. But Red Shirt was the largest, over three miles long. Most of the lakes were connected by creeks and portages, and the area was sheltered from most wind. Red Shirt Lake used to be called *Tanltun Bena*, and was known for the trout that could be caught through the ice. Some Knik families held their spring camp on both sides of the mouth of Lynx Creek. Others came here for summer fish camp. It was a good area for lynx, marten, beaver, and otter, too.

The people had been coming here for a long, long time, longer than even Cheeda could remember. The proof of their presence was the number of house pits in the surrounding forest. House pits were the remains of the partially underground houses the people had lived in, warm and cozy, before they had learned from Russian trappers how to build log cabins. Their old *nichil* were built over three-foot-deep pits dug in the ground, and then topped with domed roofs covered with sod. The roofs were strong enough that children could walk on them.

The children enjoyed playing in these house pits, pretending they were grownup homeowners, stirring the ancient charcoal of old fireplaces, and bedding down in the little bedroom pits attached to the big main room.

The landscape here was dense with spruce and birch, aspen and willow. There were many low-brush bogs and areas of muskeg too wet for trees to grow. Wild blue iris and yellow water lilies flourished in this lake country.

When Chief Stephen's family arrived, the second chief of Susitna Station, Red Shirt himself, was already here. Red Shirt was a famous trapper who had the biggest smoke house on the lake, and two big copper cooking buckets. He loved visitors and exchanging stories. Often he had his wife bake all their flour into bread. Then he would go around the lake and gather all the young children, carrying the littlest ones back to his house on his back. There he would feed them all the bread they could hold, and then tell them stories.

Olga set down her heavy bundle with a sigh of relief. She noticed that pussy willows were blooming at the ends of their branches ten feet above ground where the spring sun had reached them. Stephen began shoveling out access to the cabin door.

As soon as camp was set up, Chief Stephen and John renewed their muskrat snares. Small, sleek muskrats were now beginning to leave their burrows deep under the lake banks to look for fresh food. Muskrats used the same burrows year after year, so Stephen and John knew where to look.

The next day, Stephen and John had five muskrats. They skinned them and saved their pelts. The pelts were not as good as marten, but everything had its use.

Olga boiled the meat of the muskrats in a birch bark basket suspended from a tripod by a hook of antler. She carefully picked up clean, hot rocks from the fire with wooden tongs and lowered them one by one into the basket of dark, raw meat and cold water. The hot rocks warmed the water and soon brought it to a boil, cooking the meat. As the rocks cooled, Olga removed them with her tongs, and heated them again in the coals of the fire. She replaced the cooled rocks with heated rocks. In this way, the clever Athapascans cooked dinner in a container that was not fireproof metal, but did not burn it. Olga's family loved the tender meat and the delicious broth in which it had cooked. They drank down the last drop.

John preferred to roast his muskrat on a stick over an open campfire. Ravens and magpies watched from the spruce trees as he put a clean piece of birchbark beneath from his spit to catch the sizzling juices as they dripped from the roasting meat. "This is better," he said, as he munched muskrat.

When they were not ice fishing or snaring muskrat, the men and boys were collecting birch bark. This outer covering of the paper birch tree was very useful to the Athapascans. It was pliable and tough. They used it for canoes, baskets, dishes, trays, roofs, and sheds for smoking fish. They curled it into cone-shaped moose calls, and, if someone broke an arm, they used it as a cast while the bone healed. The bark was loose at this time of year, as the sap began rising in the trees. It could be removed from the tree with a knife made from a sharpened caribou rib.

Once, when Olga and the family had been living here, sandhill cranes had rested on their migration. The long-legged birds with their red crowns had wingspans of six feet. Olga was fascinated with their courtship dance, a combination of head bowing, leaping into the air, and wing flapping. The big gray birds seemed to have no weight as they pranced, rose lightly into the air and landed again. That stately dance was a fond memory for Olga, something to think about at she stacked bark in a lean-to.

When the numbers of muskrats in the snares dwindled and a good supply of bark was collected and stored, it was time at last for squirrel camp, the time Olga had been anxiously awaiting.

Chapter Four

Ground Squirrel Camp

Chief Stephen and the other men of Knik were the hunters of big Alaskan game animals like moose, caribou, mountain sheep and goats, and black and brown bear. They left the season's base camp on long hunts after these prey, sometimes staying away for over a week.

But the young women and honeymooning couples were the only ones allowed to trap the ground squirrel, which they called the "parky squirrel" because its thick pelts were so well suited to making winter jackets.

While the men of Knik remained in the village making canoes and waterproofing their seams with hot spruce pitch, the young women went to their favorite squirrel areas. After Olga and her family hiked back to Knik, Olga discussed her plans with other young women of the village. Before they left Knik, the eight squirrel hunters agreed where each couple would go, so they would not trespass on one another's hunting grounds. By heading to a variety of locations, all would have good hunting, and there would be plenty of squirrels year after year.

"Gronia and I will go to the Talkeetnas," Olga said.

The Talkeetnas are a low ridge of mountains just north of Cook Inlet and Knik, the first of several ridges of foothills which eventually rise, two hundred miles north, to Mount McKinley or "Denali," "the great one," tallest peak in North America.

When the pair of hunters had agreed on their destinations, all began to pack for the journey.

A ground squirrel at its burrow is watchful.

"I will bring my knife, and some flint to start fires, and some dried wild cotton for tinder," Olga said, as she piled these objects on a large square of cloth which she would knot into a bundle to sling onto her back.

"I will bring my new birchbark pot for cooking squirrel meat," said Gronia, Olga's twelve-year-old sister. Gronia had made her new pot with a contrasting decoration of darker bark, cut in a jagged border. "And some sinew. And strips of *balik* from the cache." *Balik* was dried salmon from summer fish camp. It was good food for a journey.

"Remember extra socks," Matrona said, coming through the doorway of Olga's cabin with a pair of new fur mittens for Gronia. "It is sure to be wet there on the mountain slopes, and you will get your feet wet. And I will lend you my dog Copper to pack your extra gear, and keep watch over your camp."

"I will need forty good, big, thick skins to make my

husband's new parky," Olga said. "Isn't that right, Mother?"

"Yes," Matrona replied, "and two extras in case your knife should nick them and make a hole when you sew."

At age thirty-four, Matrona was the best skin sewer in the whole village of Knik. The men in her family were lucky to have such a fine seamstress to care for them. Good clothing helped to keep them healthy, and kept them warm when they were hunting.

"The best part of making a parky is trapping the ground squirrels in the mountains," said Olga enthusiastically.

Ground squirrel camp usually took place near the end of April, when the adult male squirrels began to tunnel out of the hard, drifted snow that had been piling up since late August over their deep burrows in the steep limestone and granite slopes.

Each woman thought she knew the best mountain passes, the best rocky slopes where the biggest colonies of squirrels lived. Olga looked forward to spring squirrel camp as if it were a vacation. True, it was a break from her usual chores at Knik village. But, there would be plenty of work at squirrel camp, and the girls knew there was danger, too. Bears like to eat ground squirrel meat as much as people did. Grizzlies would spend hours digging up large patches of tundra with their sharp claws, sending gravel flying as they tried to reach a squirrel in its deep burrow. Still, Olga could hardly wait to get started on the long trail to Hatcher Pass.

Now everything was ready.

"Goodbye, Michael, my dear little Mishka," said Olga fondly as she hugged her son, now twenty-five months old, very close. While she was away, Mishka would be cared for by his half-sister Nellie, six, by her mother,

Matrona, and by her husband's mother, old, bent
Grandma Stephen. "Goodbye, Cheeda," she said.

Olga and Gronia hoisted their heavy bundles and set
off, accompanied by Matrona's dog Copper and Gronia's
dog Tiqin, or "Wolf." As soon as they left the village,
it seemed very quiet. They could hear Cottonwood Creek
gurgling among the trees.

At first Olga and Gronia walked along a mining trail,
a narrow road cut through the stunted spruce woods.
Along this muddy track horses and sledges dragged gold
mining equipment and timbers for shafts that Herning,
the Knik storekeeper, and other prospectors had dug
deep into the earth. So early in the year, the track was
firm, frozen into unyielding, icy ruts.

After two hours, when they had walked nearly eight
miles, they reached a beautiful birch wood, the black
branches of the gleaming white trunks still bare of
leaves. There were still deep snow drifts in the most
shaded spots on both sides of the trail.

Suddenly two huge moose stepped from the shadows
and crossed the trail, making almost no noise. They were
bulls, seven feet tall at the shoulders, shaggy, but without antlers. The girls knew the moose had shed their
great racks in the darkest part of the year. They looked
but could see no sign of the new set which the moose
would begin to sprout in May.

Tiqin lunged forward, ready to chase the shaggy,
high-stepping animals. Copper, who was carrying a
heavy pack slung on both sides of his back, knew better.

"No, Tiqin!" exclaimed Gronia quietly, grabbing the
dog's loose coat and struggling to hold him back.
"Moose could kill you with one kick!" she whispered.
"Their long legs could walk right over you as if you were
a tiny pebble!"

"They could hurt us, too," whispered Olga, as the moose paused to look at the humans and their dogs. The girls tried to stay very still. Copper was well trained; he stood baring his teeth, but did not make a sound.

After a few long minutes, the moose vanished quietly down a narrow animal track into an alder thicket. The two girls let out two sighs of relief.

It took two days of walking to reach the rocky foothills of the Talkeetnas at Hatcher Pass, north of the deep canyon of the muddy Matanuska River. Part of the trail paralleled the banks of the Little Susitna, a river that tumbled over big boulders in green and blue waves. The dancing waters were very different from the gray, salty tides of Cook Inlet. The girls paused to drink deep of the ice cold water and to remove their mukluks and rub their sore feet.

Olga with the dogs, Copper and Tiqin, loaded for the trip to ground squirrel camp.

The girls were tired but excited as they climbed closer to Hatcher Pass. For the last two or three miles, as the trees grew further apart and finally gave way to dry grasses and last summer's wild celery stalks poking through the snow, the trail was steep and icy. The air was colder here as it slipped off the white peaks and through the high Talkeetna passes where squirrel colonies pocked the slopes. Now Olga and Gronia could see the channels of the Matanuska far below.

"This is a good place," said Olga finally, as she dropped her bundle in a last thicket of alders. There were no permanent cabins at squirrel camp. The sisters would live in a kind of temporary trail shelter called a ground-squirrel house. Some squirrel camp couples used the new canvas tents, but Olga preferred the traditional shelter. To make it, the girls bent down young alders and tied them together at the top in such a way as to form a small, round dome. Over the dome they tied moose skins they had brought, and heaped snow on top of that. This type of shelter gave good protection from the wind and cold, but did not attract the attention of bears. It looked much like a large tundra hummock.

Olga did not envy the new canvas tents from the Knik trading post, for the tents were not as warm as the old-fashioned, snow-insulated shelters. And the canvas was heavy to carry. The shelters were built on the spot and could be left behind.

"Now let us set our snares," said Olga, and she and Gronia began to set out snares at the mouths of all the burrows in the area. When they were hungry, they returned to camp to eat, sitting back to back on a big, dry pillow of broken alder boughs. The sisters sat this way because it was warm and friendly, and because they could survey the whole pass, keeping watch for bears.

Shoulder to shoulder, they could see much of the territory they had traveled over, and sometimes imagined they could see all the way to Knik.

For their first meal at Hatcher Pass, the girls had hot China tea and *balik*. "Tomorrow," Olga told Gronia, swallowing her last bit of dried salmon, "we will feast on boiled *qunsha*. Remember from camp last year? How juicy and tasty those *qunsha* are?"

"Um, do I!" said Gronia, who was growing fast and always hungry. "I'll eat one by myself."

"Maybe—with the help of Tiqin," Olga said with a smile to herself, picturing a fat, two-pound squirrel that even greedy Gronia would find too much for dinner.

Down below, in the Matanuska River valley and along the shores of Cook Inlet, spring was in the air. But at this altitude of 4,200 feet, with great Lynx Peak rising another 2,000 feet nearby to block the sun, it was wintery still.

Here alpine lakes were often still covered with ice in July, and little spring blizzards would suddenly blast down over the peaks and take the sisters by surprise.

During these squalls, they would huddle in their tiny shelter. They were glad to have *qunsha* and snowshoe hare blankets to wrap about themselves, and warm caribou skin mukluks with tough moosehide soles to protect their feet. Inside the knee-high mukluks they wore socks of hare or ground squirrel fur. Over their mittens, they wore outer gauntlet gloves with deep, flaring cuffs that covered half their lower arms. The gauntlets were sewn of moosehide, large and clumsy, but very warm. When they tugged off the heavy gauntlets to remove squirrels from their snares, braided ropes of bright red yarn prevented the girls from losing their gloves. Each yarn braid was stitched to a gauntlet cuff and then passed behind the neck.

"How the sun glares on the snow, Olga," complained Gronia at noon one day, tugging her parky hood forward to shade her eyes, and rubbing the sore lids with the backs of her hands. Both sisters were squinting against the glare. The strong spring sun was tanning them, too. "Soon our faces will be as dark brown and rough as Matrona's and Cheeda's. We will look just like the best parky makers." The sisters smiled at each other with pride.

All day as they worked they heard the scolding chatter of male *qunsha* who peered from the earthen doorways of their newly, opened burrows or ran darting from grassy hummocks, trying to stay out of sight of the humans, but curious about them at the same time. Now and again Olga and Gronia glimpsed their scurrying tawny or dark brown bodies, and were glad to know that there were many more squirrels to be caught. The squirrels called and called, seeming to say, "Sik-sik! Sik-sik!" "That's what the Eskimos call *qunsha*," Olga said. "They call them 'sik-sik puk'."

The small opening to a burrow, with its mound of freshly dug earth drying in the sun, tells little of what the burrow is like inside the mountain slope. Each narrow opening leads five to eight feet into the mountainside, ending in a sleeping den nine or ten inches in diameter. Before their long winter naps, the squirrels line their dens with dry grass. By spring they have absorbed all the extra fat they gained in late summer, preparing for sleep. So when they emerge from their burrows, the hungry squirrels, now in loose coats that seem too big for them, rush about seeking tender stems, leaves, seeds, insects and birds' eggs to eat. The big gray squirrels, eighteen inches from blunt nose to furry rump, were easy for the girls to spot against the melting white drifts. In their haste to find food, many squirrels stumbled into snares and were caught fast.

Snaring the animals was only part of the girls' work. The squirrels they snared had to be skinned and gutted the same day, to keep the valuable pelts in the best condition.

Sunset would find the tired sisters sitting and skinning, back to back on their home-made pillow of alder boughs. Tiny movements of their sharp curved women's knives, or *ulus*, showed the care they took. There were lines of concentration around their dark brown eyes as they worked. It would not do to have unnecessary cuts in the furs. The girls worked the pelts back off the bodies from nose to tail, as if turning a tight brown sock off a deep pink foot. They tried to scrape off every bit of flesh that could rot and spoil the fur. Then they strung a thin piece of rawhide string called *babiche* through the eyeholes and hung the skins up like identical pieces of laundry. The mountain wind dried the fresh furs well. When a rawhide "clothesline" contained forty dry skins, it was taken down, tied into a bundle and stored in the shelter.

Olga and Gronia had set a high goal for themselves. Each was trying to collect five bundles, or 200 skins, so the men and big boys of their households would have warm parkys. The thickest, most beautiful skins would be saved for dress parkies. These brought prestige to the owner and his family. Dress parkies were worn on Russian Orthodox church holidays and other special occasions, such as feasts in honor of ancestors who had died but were still remembered with respect. At ancestors' feast, there were big pots of moose soup and other deli-

*Beaded mittens are worn on special occasions, and are
decorated in typical Athapascan style.*

cious food. Gronia licked her lips when she thought of ancestors' feasts. She dreamed of the beaded mittens she would wear for the dancing.

Day after tiring day, the two sisters set their spruce root snares, skinned squirrels, chewed cold boiled squirrel meat, and drank hot squirrel broth. Night after long, cold night they folded new innersoles of dry grass for their mukluks, and they cuddled together lovingly in their tiny shelter. Hot rocks, laid on green willow boughs, kept the shelter cozy at night.

While the sisters worked, Gronia's dog, Tiqin, stalked marmots. Much larger than ground squirrels, as big as Tiqin himself, marmots enjoy teasing dogs. Their long, golden hair standing up in the morning fog, the marmots whistled shrill warning to one another, and the warnings echoed tantalizingly from the surrounding peaks. Tiqin would whirl and chase. But he always seemed to be chasing an echo, darting in the wrong direction, or just missing the big marmot he was after. The marmot would dive into a tangle of boulders or ooze into its burrow just out of the dog's reach. Then another marmot would pop up a few yards away, and Tiqin was off again, until his tongue was hanging out with the effort. When the muscular gray dog tired of this marmot chase, he headed back to camp where there were always plenty of squirrel bones for him to crunch.

"Silly dog," said Olga, patting Tiqin. She had seen him whirl and chase in just his way at squirrel camp the year before.

Gronia always kept a few squirrel bones for herself. Squirrel leg bones made excellent sewing needles, and extra bone needles could be taken to the trading post and exchanged for sugar, tea or yarn. Gronia enjoyed going to Herning's store and looking at the strange things on the shelves.

Chapter Five

Legend of the Twisted Snare

One night, as the wind howled around their shelter, Olga stacked the bundles of cured furs around the edges to make it warmer. She pulled her hare blanket close under her chin, and began to tell Gronia three *Dghiliq' sukdu'a,* stories Athapascans tell only when they are hunting in the mountains. This is the third of the "mountain stories" Olga told sleepy Gronia as they snuggled together in their shelter on the slopes of Hatcher Pass:

"Before the world as we know it began, all animals were human. They looked just like people. Some of them, like Raven and Lynx and Wolverine, could change; they would do some things in animal form, and some things in human form in those days we are talking about. (And you know, Gronia, even today, if you skin a bear, he looks just like a man.) These animal-people had canoes, kayaks, and sleds. They used bows and arrows and cooking pots. They lived in warm houses, and they walked upright.

"And the animals and humans talked to one another, in the same language, with words both understood perfectly, and they visited one another's homes like honored guests.

"Two women regularly hunted ground squirrels in the mountains in early spring, before all the snow had left the peaks. It was hard work, but they enjoyed being away from the routine of the village. One woman was

31

older. But although she sometimes had stiff joints in the morning and moved slowly, her hair was still brown as a moose's coat, and she always snared the biggest, fattest squirrels. The other woman, who was younger and quick as an ermine in her neat movements, snared only the small squirrels. Sometimes she felt jealous of her older sister's skill.

"One day the younger woman was lost in the cold mist and fog of the peaks. No warming sun worked through the fog that morning. As she stumbled and slipped on the ice-glazed rocks and the slimy grasses of the hummocks, weighed down by her bundles of snares and fresh squirrels, a huge female ground squirrel appeared and spoke to her. She invited the younger sister into her home with sweet, welcoming words.

"Come, lay down your bundles. Come with me, young woman! You are tired. Come rest your feet. I have dry grass for new innersoles," coaxed the mother squirrel, bowing slightly and avoiding eye contact in the most polite and refined manner.

"The tired young woman let herself be persuaded," said Olga, "especially when the squirrel offered her a piece of wild, green celery—even though the snow was still on the ground and the new celery sprouts were not yet visible anywhere. Chewing on the juicy, peeled celery stalk, the young woman crawled into the squirrel's warm burrow, which was as large as a chief's house. There were no glass windows, but there was a fire in the burrow, a fire of dry birch and spruce logs, circled by rocks to confine it. And there was a clean birch bark cup of spruce needle tea waiting on a flat stone. The squirrel woman handed the tea to her young guest.

"As the young woman sipped the pungent tea, she looked more closely at the burrow. She was amazed at its comforts. The walls were lined with beautifully woven grass mats. She hesitantly reached out a finger to touch the woven design on the wall nearest her.

"Then the woman heard a strangled whimper from the shadows behind her. Turning around, startled, she saw a baby ground squirrel with a snare tight around his waist. The twisted snare cut off his breath, and he gasped, in great pain. Tears poured from his beautiful eyes, wetting the soft fur of his cheeks."

Gronia began to snore lightly, but Olga nudged her awake, and continued her story.

"The cup of tea fell from the young woman's hand as she recognized the twisted snare as her own. Because of her jealousy of her sister's talents, she had marked all her snares with a tuft of wiry moosehair, dyed red. Delicately she loosened the snare and slipped it off, and the baby stopped crying at once. He could once more breathe normally.

"Thank you, young woman," said the polite child, who then lay down to sleep on a mat before the fire, exhausted. His life had been saved.

"When the sun burned the thick mist from the mountain side beyond the burrow's entrance, the young woman crawled from the cozy den, thanking the squirrel mother as she left.

"From that day forward," Olga said, "she snared only big male squirrels, and her sewing got better and better, her stitches tinier and tinier." Now that the story was over, both girls settled down to sleep.

Olga remembered many mountain stories that her mother had told her on past visits to the pass to snare squirrels. Telling them to Gronia helped to pass the cold evenings. Gronia enjoyed them all and learned much about the ways of her people.

In a little over two weeks, the busy sisters had harvested four bundles of furs each, plus others for socks.
Leftover squirrel meat had been dried in the wind and
sun to make jerky for the relatives back in Knik. Jerky
was valuable food when there was no fresh meat or fish.

The sisters had seen no bears during the day, although
they knew there were bear trails ground into the tops of
the ridges above the pass. Generations of bears stepping
in one another's footsteps had created trails several
inches deep and as wide as John's arm was long.

Late one evening when Olga and Gronia least ex-
pected it, they heard pebbles fall. Looking up in the
direction of the noise, they saw a thin, confused grizzly,
fresh from hibernation, searching for ground squirrels to
eat. As the hungry bear picked his way down the slope
of loose rock, his keen nose sniffed the sweet breeze from
the sisters' "clothesline" of drying furs and meat. He put
his nose into the air and swiveled his head right and left,
right and left, trying to pinpoint the source. His talented
nose made up for his poor eyesight, and he headed right
for their camp. Armed only with short skinning knives
and *ulus,* Olga and Gronia turned to each other with
fear.

Copper was off chasing marmots. But Tiqin was on
guard. When the dog barked frantically, and made short
charges in the bear's direction, the young grizzly turned
away and lumbered down toward the Little Susitna
River. He decided to avoid a battle with this loud barker
and his human companions. The girls were relieved and
grateful to Tiqin, rubbing his head and ears to show him
what a good dog he had been. If Tiqin had not fright-
ened the bear away, the grizzly could have destroyed all
the results of their weeks of work.

Now it was May, and the female and yearling squirrels were emerging from their dens lower down on the slopes of Hatcher Pass. The males that the sisters preferred to snare stopped lolling about their snowy front yards, and began running and fighting with one another, competing for mates. During these battles, they often tore holes in their loose coats, making their pelts useless for dress parkys.

"I can see the pale green down below," said Olga to Gronia sadly one morning as the sun rose. She knew the pale green was a haze of new leaves spreading through the cottonwood, alder and birch in the valley below, along the banks of the Matanuska and Knik Rivers. This meant they needed to return to their village. So they packed up their camp, and, heavily loaded down, retraced the long trail to Knik.

Much of the trail was muddy now with water from melting snow. They paused many times to rest because of the weight of their loads, but they did not see any moose on their return. Moose could now find food at higher elevations.

Chapter Six

Home Again

Fat and jolly, Olga's baby son Michael was squatting in a pile of wood chips, tossing them into his shining black hair when the two sisters walked into the village. At first Michael did not seem to remember his mother, and looked for his grandmother Matrona nervously, wondering who this tanned stranger was. But when Olga spoke to him in a soft, cooing voice that she often used with her baby, he screeched with delight, and toddled to her, hugging her knees with his short, pudgy arms. At the screech, Matrona came rushing around the corner of her cabin to see what mischief he was into now. When she saw the girls, she knew it was a false alarm.

"Greetings, my daughters," Matrona said to Olga and Gronia as they wearily set down their bundles and began to remove the dogs' packs. "I see you have the makings of many parkies. Your time at squirrel camp was well spent." This was high praise indeed from Matrona, and the girls were pleased to hear it.

Grandmother Stephen decided to make berry pudding to celebrate her granddaughters' successful hunting trip and safe return. Berry pudding was a new dish that the Athapascans had learned to make since sugar and flour had been introduced into the country.

From her cache Cheeda took dried high bush and low bush cranberries and rose hips, the fruit of the prickly wild rose. She put these wrinkled red fruits into a new

Michael, whom Olga left behind while she hunted squirrels, plays with wood chips.

cast iron pot and added clean water. Then Cheeda hung the pot over a fire in the yard, and when the dried berries were soft and the mixture was bubbling, she stirred in a little white sugar. When the sugar had dissolved, flour was added, whisked in with a bunch of clean birch twigs tied together at one end. The flour thickened the pudding, and soon Cheeda had a tasty, sweet, red mush, which she dished out with a ladle Grandfather Stephen had carved for her from alder. Alder was one wood that did not add a strange taste to food it touched.

For a little while the sisters enjoyed the luxury of sitting and resting, eating the edges of their sweet pudding as it cooled in wooden bowls, laughing and telling of their adventures in the mountains, of the ptarmigan they had seen beginning to change color and the fresh willow leaves they had eaten on the walk back to Knik. After the long winter with no greens, fresh willow leaves made a wonderful snack to pluck and eat while walking.

Food and supplies are kept in these storage houses or "caches" to prevent bears and other animals from stealing valuables.

But no one in Knik rested for long. There was always work to be done, and Chief Stephen's new parky was far from finished. Although the sisters had snared, cleaned and dried the ground squirrel skins, the skins needed a great deal more work before sewing could begin.

Early the following day, Gronia and Olga turned all their skins fur side in, moistening them with a little oily water left from boiling dried fish for dinner. Gronia had some flour from the Knik Station store across Knik Arm, and that she made into a thin paste. She rubbed the flour paste carefully on the insides of her pelts.

Caterina and some of the other children watched idly. Caterina was often as hungry for food as her older sister Gronia. She hated to see costly flour used for tanning pelts just when she was wishing for pancakes! Olga wisely removed the grumbling Caterina and her friends Simeon and Theodore by sending them into the forest to gather a flour sack of willow buds. That would keep them out of her hair, and make an extra dish for dinner.

When all the skins were moistened with flour paste, each was turned right side out, rolled up, and left in a cool place over night.

Bright and early the next morning, work began again. The skins were unrolled one at a time, turned wrong side out, then right side out, over and over again, to soften them.

Gronia, Olga and Matrona worked side by side. The women had no choice but to keep turning and kneading the squirrel pelts for the entire spring morning. Everyone helped when not busy with other chores, even Cheeda, although her hands were very stiff.

That afternoon Gronia climbed the long ladder of the chief's cache, a raised storage shed the size of a small log cabin. The cache was raised on ten-foot legs to keep it out of reach of wolverines and other raiders. Inside the cache were some stretchers made of flat pieces of wood, carved by the men during past winters. The older children were sent to gather willow branches, thin and supple, to make other frames or stretchers, one for each skin. Although Olga had strong hands, she could stretch only half a bundle of furs a day onto stretchers. It was very hard work.

This stretching continued for several days, until all the fresh ground squirrel pelts were slipped onto stretchers so that they would dry flat.

When they were dry, the skins were peeled from their stretchers and kneaded between the palms like balls of clay until they were soft and pliable as a ball of knitting yarn. Then they were put onto the stretchers again, and leaned against the shady side of the cabin. All the cabins in the village had their rows of stretched skins, for the women who had gone to squirrel camps in the surrounding foothills had now all returned to Knik.

Day after day work continued with the squirrel skins, until all the furs were perfectly soft, dry, and flat. Then they were stored away in bundles of forty, in the caches, which were now empty of moose, caribou, and bear meat, and echoed like flat stomachs when their heavy log doors were shut fast.

The women were relieved to have this part of the season over and done with.

All this time Chief Stephen and the other men of Knik had been repairing their birchbark boats, mending their willow nets, replacing sinkers, inspecting their fish hooks and lines, and steaming and bending wood to make new hooks. They must be ready for the next camp of the year.

The birch leaves, which had been smaller than Michael's small thumbnail, grew bigger and darker green. Soon they were larger than a raven's beak, then as big as a magpie breast feather. The leaves seemed to fill up the forest where there had been nothing but empty branches just weeks before. Fireweed pierced the damp earth with its dark red and green shoots. Cottonwoods and trembling aspen sent out new leaves, too, and then the prickly wild roses began to bloom in the first week of June.

Chapter Seven

Summer Fish Camp

Chief Stephen's people did not live in the same place all year round, but moved from camp to camp, following the food supplies of different seasons. Now it was time for fish camp. Several Knik families chose as their fish camp Tyonek, where the shore sloped down to a stony beach. Their families had gone to this spot every summer as long as anyone could remember. Other families took their boats to Fire Island. At fish camp, the people would catch and dry salmon.

The people camped in canvas tents or in rough shelters of bark over driftwood frames. Fishing season after fishing season, they used the same timber frameworks with loose bark roofs. These were the smoke houses used for preserving their catch. On the scraped ground beneath these bark roofs, Cheeda and Caterina and other women and children kept small fires going day and night. Salmon strips were hung to smoke and could be kept drying even if it began to rain.

The morning after the family reached fish camp, John rose early. He wanted to catch the first salmon of the year. Sure enough, before anyone else was even stirring, he pulled in a fish that weighed eight pounds.

When Chief Stephen came to the beach, John was waiting quietly to present him with the glistening fish. The chief called everyone else: "Get up, our brother has come to visit us," he said in a loud voice. "Our brother is here. We must greet our long-lost brother."

43

The other Knik families were excited that salmon were running in Cook Inlet again. When everyone was gathered, the fish was given a drink of fresh water from a cup before it was cooked. Then everyone in the camp ate a little piece of that first salmon. To show that they were grateful for the fish's coming, its bones were thrown back into the salty water of Cook Inlet, and Chief Stephen said a prayer:

> *O fish,*
> *We have treated you nicely,*
> *O brother from the sea.*
> *You are so delicious.*
> *You help us to live.*
> *We return your bones*
> *To the water you came from.*
> *Grow pink flesh again on these white bones.*
> *Then come again to help us live.*
> *You are welcome here, brother.*
> *Come back to us again, O fish.*

After the chief's solemn prayer, everyone in camp began catching salmon with dip nets and hooks. Matrona, Cheeda and Gronia began preparing the catch for drying and smoking. They called this "cutting fish." Matrona left the two halves of the fish attached just below the tail, so the halves could hang on either side of the drying rack. But she removed the backbone in one piece. Her curved knife cut along the bones cleanly as if cutting through bear grease in a bark bucket. Many fish camps, many years of practice, had given Matrona this skill and speed, so that nothing was wasted of the precious food. The magpies who came to pick at the cast off backbones found little nourishment there.

As she cut fish, Matrona reviewed the protocols of caring for salmon with Gronia and the other young women.

"Remember, you must use care," Matrona said, her knife not pausing for a moment. "The bones must be kept in one piece and thrown back into the water. If one tiny bone is missing, the salmon may not return next year."

She looked toward the shadowy glades of the forest, from which John and Simeon were just emerging with large, green bundles. These were fresh fern fronds.

"We must clean the fish with ferns, not with water. We must cut the first salmon with a stone knife, and the cuts must be up and down, not cross-wise." Her knife cleanly followed the directions indicated by her words. "And we must pluck out the heart and burn it in the fire. If we follow these paths of respect, the salmon will put flesh on these bones and return to us again."

John and Simeon put their bundles down next to the toiling women and girls and drew near to hear what Matrona was saying.

"The salmon never dies," she said. "Once salmon were not fish at all, but people who lived in a big village under the water. They had warm houses and plenty of firewood cut. These salmon people liked humans, and showed their love by sending their young men and women disguised as fish to meet the humans and be food in their pots and *balik* on their racks. They came willingly to be put up."

"If we show our respect," she continued, "and treat their bodies gently and put their bones back into the water, they will become delicious, fat fish again in their home villages."

Matrona, Olga and the other women worked from sunrise to sunset during these long, long summer days.

Women slice and clean the salmon and hang them up to dry on fish racks at the summer fish camp.

Matrona could fillet more than a thousand salmon a day. Some days she cut 120 an hour. Matrona had been cutting fish since she was eleven—but oh, how her shoulders ached each evening!

One morning Matrona looked up from her fish cutting and noticed John had a frog in his grimy hand. "Come here, John," said Matrona in a quiet voice, her *ulu* poised in mid-air. "When you find a frog near the house, put it in a container, in a piece of rag, and return it to the forest. Long ago, when the world began, that frog was a person who lived in a beautiful house with glass windows. He is a living thing," she told John. "He must get scared when big human boys come near him. You should apologize and treat him nicely. All things— bears, fish, marten, even frogs—have spirits and must be respected. You must show respect even for the logs for the fire."

John was sorry he had forgotten his manners, and did as Matrona said with his young cousin, the frog.

Because of a shallow swamp of stagnant water just behind Tyonek beach, mosquitoes were very bad at fish camp. The people smeared mud over their faces and legs to discourage the biting insects and went on with their work. Those who tended the fires had the best of it, for the smoke discouraged mosquitoes.

Despite bug bites and endless fish, fish, fish, everyone enjoyed fish camp. There was plenty of salmon, salmon eggs, seaweed, and the roots of chocolate lilies to eat. The children learned at only three or four years old how to recognize the lily plant, with its brown flower. They used sticks to dig up the roots, and brought them to their mothers. When boiled, the white roots looked like rice.

Late one evening, at the time when night animals begin to stir, John found a porcupine chewing on the wooden handle of a woman's slate knife that had been carelessly left on the ground near a smoke house. The porky was enjoying the handle because the wood had a salty taste from long use. In summer, John knew, porkies are fat and tasty. He easily clubbed the slow, sluggish animal over the head with a big piece of driftwood.

Next morning, Matrona complimented John on his successful hunt. "This is a nice big one, John. It is good to have sharp-eyed young hunters walking the trails and bringing home game."

Matrona examined the three-foot porky. She pulled out many of its stiff, barbed quills and stored them in a bag made of a pelican's pouch. The quills would be dyed, flattened between her teeth and sewn onto summer caribou skin tunics in colorful borders.

Then Matrona prepared to make porcupine stew—a nice change from salmon. It is difficult to skin a porcupine without having sharp quills hook into your skin, so Matrona let flame do the work for her. She built a large fire in the open. Then she laid across it several heavy, wet, green poles. She lifted the thirty-five-pound porky with sticks, and laid it crosswise on the poles. Matrona did not allow her attention to wander, except to keep Michael from toddling near the fire. She did not want the meat to burn. The porcupine was turned several times, to allow the flickering tongues of flame to reach all parts of the body, until the sharp quills, wooly fur and skin were charred away.

The carcass was then removed to some nearby beach rocks to cool, and a young neighbor was assigned to keep the dogs away. "Come, Dolly," called Matrona to one of the little girls of the village. "You are five now and can do this work. Do not let Copper, Tiqin and the other dogs steal the meat for our dinner." Dolly found a limber branch for hitting the nose of any dogs that came too close, and took up a guard post on a nearby boulder. She practiced waving her branch about her, and the dogs kept their distance.

When the meat had cooled, Matorna gutted the porcupine with quick, sure strokes of her curved knife, saving the liver and heart to fry and keeping the large intestines. She cut the porky into bite-size chunks, washed them and put them into her pot to cook. She washed the intestines well, braided them and added the braid to the pot with the cleaned head, short tail and feet.

All morning the porky stew simmered, sending delicious smells on the breeze to the fishermen on the beach. As they gulped porky at noon, everyone nodded approval to Matrona, the cook, and to John, the hunter.

The children loved fish camp. They had chores, of course, like gathering enough driftwood for drying each day's catch. But when their chores were finished, they could play with their cousins who spent the winter at Tyonek. On the swamp flats, they learned to know the yellow flowers and lacy, gray-green leaves of *k'tl'ila* (Indian potatoes) and eagerly dug up as many as they could find. The boys practiced spearing salmon trying to swim upstream to spawn at Chakachamna Lake.

Many families gathered at fish camp. Some fishermen at Tyonek came from as far away as Copper River, two-hundred miles by foot. In the cool evenings, the adults enjoyed dancing, feasting and giggling about weddings that would take place in the future. There was even time for more riddles.

Simeon created this riddle:

My nose works so hard to smell
The river where I was born
That it grows around, it curves around
To pinch my chin.
I grow thin
With worry and travel.
I make my nest in gravel.
Who am I?

It took John just seconds to guess the answer—the spawning salmon, whose heads and bodies change shape as they race from the Pacific Ocean to the places where they hatched from eggs laid in gravel nests three or four years before.

During the summer, John had been thinking about the tides of Cook Inlet, and the action of the Matanuska and Knik Rivers and other freshwater streams that flowed into Cook Inlet and then into the vast Pacific. So he made this riddle:

I am a carver.
I cut out little bits,
But I can also put bits back when I choose.
I change the shape of the world.
I carve without a knife.
I live alone:
No house, no cache, no dog, no wife.
Who am I?

John's riddle had Simeon stumped for an entire morning, but then the younger boy came up with the answer: a river. The river took away from the shore, but it also built sand bars.

All too soon the salmon were gone. Now only their yawning skeletons lay among the granite and quartz cobbles at the edges of the spawning streams. The season of fish camp was over. The children, all of whom seemed to have grown several inches after these months in the warm sun with plenty of good food, had to say goodbye to their cousins for another year.

Chapter Eight

Berries and Beluga

Late August was time for berry camp, and the people of Knik moved once more in search of food. This time they moved further south on the west shore of Cook Inlet, to some high hills with south-facing slopes near Tyonek. On these slopes above treeline, the warm summer sun had ripened blueberries and mossberries early.

One morning Olga, who was expecting a new baby in the spring, felt sleepy. She balanced her berry bucket carefully between two hummocks and lay down for a short nap in the soft, fragrant heather. But suddenly something woke her, a sound of heavy breathing with bird-like twittering. She knew it could not be a chickadee or a swallow. She sat up and peered over the edge of the slope to find out what was making the strange combination of sounds.

Something huge and white had been stranded on the beach by the high tide of the Inlet. Still drowsy, Olga thought at first that it was a merchant's ship from Seattle, headed to Knik docks with sugar, plaid cloth, and shiny metal needles. Then she realized this was no white sail, but something much better for her people, a beluga, a white whale. She rose to her feet.

"*Quyusi*," she shouted as loudly as she could. "*Quyusi! Hhuk!*" which in Tanaina Athapascan means, "Beluga! Hurry!"

"*Quyusi!*" Olga shouted again, almost tripping on her long green cotton calico skirt, and everyone stumbled

From the slopes above the inlet, Olga spies a beached whale.

gleefully down the brushy slopes carpeted with berry bushes and dwarf birch, the children's baskets spilling berries, their lips stained dark blue from their snacking. The tide of Cook Inlet had been thirty feet high, tempting this small whale to swim too far into shallow areas after a last school of salmon. When the tide went out again, the salmon escaped easily. But the larger whale could not follow and became stranded. He struggled in the gray pudding of mud and chirped like a song bird, but he could not budge his great weight.

Beluga can grow to eighteen feet long. This sleek, graceful white whale was sixteen feet in length, a welcome gift of food from the sea. The people tied ropes around the beluga's tail, and pulled it onto the rocky beach of Tyonek. The stones rumbled under their feet as they pulled hard together. Half a dozen men with knives cut up the whale, giving pieces to every family.

That evening everyone ate boiled beluga. Beluga oil dripped down their chins as they chewed beluga skin and blubber in a great, happy whale picnic on the beach.

In the days that followed, the villagers dried beluga meat over their salmon smudge fires and rendered its blubber into oil, storing the nutritious oil in bentwood boxes, barrels, the hollow stems of bulb kelp, and other containers. They needed the rich oil for winter. The oil contained vitamins and fat, necessary to keep the people healthy. During the long winter they would dip dried roots and dried salmon into the oil before eating them. This softened the dried foods and made them taste better, as well as easier to chew.

Meat and oil were not the only valuable parts of the white whale. Chief Stephen's people used all parts of any animal they harvested for food, so no part of the big beluga went to waste. Stephen and the other men saved the bones for tools. Matrona, Olga, Gronia, Cheeda and the other women saved the sinew, a tough material that connected muscles and bones. When the sinew dried, it would be split into thin strips for sewing and making fish lines.

Twisting sinew is difficult, and young girls like Caterina practiced this task often. By the time Athapascan girls grew into women, they could twist sinew in the dark, without seeing it, saving the daylight hours for sewing.

When the beluga had been stored away, it was back to the berry patches. Whenever Olga napped in the heather, she dreamed about the completed parky. As August slipped into September, she could see the parky more and more clearly in her dreams. She had her red dye now.

She had her soft, warm squirrel skins. The beluga was lucky for her parky plans, too, because beluga contained sinew. Olga and the other skin sewers of Knik liked sinew from along the backbone of the caribou best, because it was easier to work with. But beluga sinew was stronger—although harder to split into narrow individual "threads." They were always happy to have a supply of beluga sinew in their sewing kits.

For sewing parkys the sinew was twisted into pieces twelve to fourteen inches long, and then tied into neat little bundles. The traditional Athapascan and Eskimo needles had no eyes or openings. The needles guided the sinew through holes in the skins. The holes were made with sharp awls made from birds' beaks or squirrels' bones.

A berry basket made of birch bark is a useful tool.

Chapter Nine

Olga Finishes the New Parky

The people had been so busy at fish camp and berry camp that summer had passed quickly. Now it was September again, the Tanaina month Athapascans call *Wonqesani*, or "half winter." Another name is "the time when antlers are torn." By this second name they describe the season when the new moose and caribou racks lose their covering of fur-like "velvet." The big animals scrape the velvet off against shrubs and trees, leaving strips of soft, torn skin dangling from the branches. This is also the season when bull moose and caribou move up from the river flats into the foothills and mountains, and hunters follow them.

In preparation for the long Alaskan winter, Caterina, Gronia, and the other girls of Knik gathered wood and stacked it into big woodpiles for winter cooking and heating. They also searched rocky clearings for little round white puffball mushrooms, and picked cranberries in sunny glades. Some of the fruit and mushrooms were eaten fresh. The remainder was dried for the snowy months when there would be no fresh food. The rose hips they gathered would be boiled to make a red tea.

If they were old enough to keep pace, and had proved themselves like John had, the boys of Knik were allowed to go hunting with their fathers. Between hunts they learned to make snowshoes and sleds. Athapascans are famous for their excellent snowshoes, and for traveling long journeys with them in the winter. Stephen's father had carried him when he was a baby all the way to Kenai to see the Russian Orthodox priest there, and be baptised. This was a famous winter journey of three hundred miles that was often spoken of by the villagers. The boys also gathered moss, which they mixed with clay and wedged between the logs of their cabins, to seal out winter's winds.

The smallest children gathered dried wild cotton and moss. Even little Michael, now two and half years old, was shown how to do this, and gathered a few handfuls of cotton, which he proudly carried to Olga. "Good, Mishka," said Olga, giving him a big smile. The cotton would be used for catching sparks when fires were started with flint. The moss was for the babies' diapers and lining the birchbark cradles that hung from the rafters of the cabins.

It had taken a year of planning and work, but finally everything was ready for making Chief Stephen's fine new parky: beluga whale sinew for thread, red and white sealskin for trim, a tough piece of hide for a thimble to protect Olga's fingers as she sewed, a sharpened ground squirrel leg bone for a needle, an awl made from moose antler with a handle of moose bone, and enough daylight to see to sew before nights grew long again. "At last, at last," thought Olga to herself.

One evening when Chief Stephen returned home from a successful mountain sheep hunt at the mineral lick above Eklutna Lake, Olga measured him for his new jacket. First she measured his hips. Then she had him stretch out both his arms, and measured from one wrist straight across his shoulders to the other wrist. This gave her the sleeve measurement.

Olga could neither read nor write. She owned neither

pencil nor paper. She marked her measurements in an ancient way—by knotting a length of rawhide. She would remember which knot marked which measurement. She kept a length of rawhide knotted with measurements for every member of the family, taking new measurements for the children as they grew. Her patterns she kept in her head. She had memorized them watching Cheeda and Matrona sew.

The chief's parky must be loose enough to trap a layer of warm air next to his body. It must be big enough that on a very cold day, when the temperature fell to twenty-five or thirty degrees below zero and moisture froze in his nostrils and on his mustache, an inner parky made of the skins of female and yearling squirrels could be worn under it.

"Stand still, please, Stephen," Olga said, as the chief grew tired of standing in one place. He was a man used to walking and being on the trail all the time. "I am not done yet," explained his wife in a soothing tone.

For the hood, Olga measured from the base of the chief's sunburned neck around the top of his head to his forehead. She measured from his chin to the collarbone for the front part of the hood, which kept the neck warm when the wind blew chill from the Inlet. The chief shrugged his shoulders. "You're tickling," he protested.

Mishka watched all this from his seat on the dirt floor, where he played with a cup and pin toy made of caribou toe bones strung on *babiche*. The *babiche* thong had a metal pin tied to one end. Mishka did not mind sitting on the floor, because Olga had carpeted it with dry spruce boughs, which made a comfortable and fragrant seat. She regularly replaced the boughs with fresh ones from the forest.

"Please stand still," Olga said again, as the chief

wiggled. Now she measured from his armpit around his muscular shoulder to his armpit again, allowing plenty of room so that he could move his arms easily and quickly when stalking game. Caribou were curious animals who might stand still as a hunter slowly approached, but mountain sheep never stood still. They leaped away so easily one imagined they could climb right up into the clouds over Pioneer Peak.

"I am done," Olga said, making her last knot. Now the chief could lie down and relax. But, of course, as soon as he was lying down, Mishka dropped his toy into a corner and jumped on his father's stomach, begging for wrestling.

"Be bear, be bear," he begged. Stephen groaned with weariness, but he became a growling grizzly and wrestled with his baby son.

The following morning Olga began to lay out her skins, using the nicest ones where they would show most—down the outside of the sleeves and in the center of the back and front. She was careful to have the hair flow from neck to shoulders, and, on the sleeves, from shoulder to wrist. This made a smooth surface. She cut a thick, glossy marten pelt into cuffs and decorative shoulder inserts.

Chief Stephen's parky would use many kinds of fur. Most of it would be sewn of the two-sided squirrel pelts, with their dangling tails like tassels decorating the outside. But around the hood went a ruff of other fur.

"This ground squirrel skin is very tough, but light and warm," explained Olga to Gronia as she sewed. "We must fit the pelts together carefully, stitching with our beluga sinew with tiny stitches. We must be careful not to cut the pelts in any way, so there will be no holes for the wind to whistle through. You see how the jacket is really two layers, double fur, because it is made up of rows of little fur 'bags'."

"Yes, I see," said Gronia. "The gray-yellow backs of the squirrels go on the outside, with their six-inch tails dangling; and the rusty-yellow bellies for the inside or lining. It's fur inside, and fur outside, too."

There were no buttons or zippers to the parky; Stephen would pull it over his head. There would be nothing to catch on underbrush as he walked the trails after game.

"What do you think about the ruff, Gronia?" asked Olga.

"A wolverine ruff is the best, of course. A wolf or wolverine ruff means the parky belongs to a great hunter, one who can kill clever wolf or fierce wolverine," Gronia replied. "Wolf is best because when frost forms on it from freezing breath and has to be pulled off, the hair does not break."

"That is true," said Olga thoughtfully. "Frost does not form on wolverine fur so the very best ruff is wolf fur with an edge of wolverine next to the face."

The chief had many fine ruffs saved from wornout parkies, but Olga was inspired to try something new— a crown-like hat instead of a ruff. The lighter in color the ruff, the more it was prized by the villagers. So she took her husband's lightest colored wolf pelt and shaped a high, impressive hat.

"My fingers are pricked and sore from stitching with this new steel needle. It goes right through my hide thimble," said Gronia. She decided she needed a stretch and a break. She got up from her seat on a tree stump before her cabin and walked the few feet to Olga's tree stump. "How are you getting along?" she asked. When

Orville Herning's trading post at Knik was a sign of the disappearance of the traditional life of Athapascans with the arrival of more white trappers and gold prospectors.

she saw the magnificent wolf hat, she gasped. "How wonderful, Olga! The chief will be the most handsome hunter in our village."

For three more days Olga sewed. Then the parky was completed and the marvelous hat stitched to fit snugly. Stephen decided to wear these new garments to Hern-

ing's trading post to sell some of his best wolf and
marten pelts. In honor of the occasion, he put on over
the parky his chief's necklace. The necklace had be-
longed to his father before him. It was a v-shaped collection of white dentalia shells, shaped like small,
hollow tusks. These dentalia were very valuable, because
they could only be traded for with tribes that lived far
away. The necklace also contained blue and brown Russian trade beads that had come all the way from Italy,
Herning had told him. Stephen knew that Italy was a
place far beyond the Talkeetnas, even further than Denali. Narrow strips of tanned moose hide were strung
between the dentalia and beads to keep the rows from
twisting out of shape, so that every prized shell and shining bead would be properly admired.

The trading post was run by Orville Herning and his
wife and son, who was about the same age as John. The
Herning family had lived at Knik for over a year now.
Herning had built the log store with two glass windows.
The store was near the docks, and had a big porch on the
front. In the summers Herning prospected for gold in
the Talkeetna Mountains near Willow Creek, but when
the ground was frozen he went into his store, cut wood,
played cards with prospectors and homesteaders, and
made pictures with a wooden box and pieces of glass.

When Herning saw how the chief looked in his new
parky, something strange happened. He used his
wooden box, which he called a camera, to take a picture
of the chief standing on the porch of his store. Herning
had never before seen such a beautiful parky, or such a
hat as Olga had made, and he knew the chief did not
wear his necklace except on special occasions, such as
ancestor's feasts. From his negative, Herning made many
postcards to sell to tourists and others who came on

Chief Stephen in the parky and hat Olga made for him, from a photograph by Orville Herning in the Anchorage Museum of History and Art collection, Anchorage, Alaska.

schooners during the summer. On the chief's next visit the following week, he gave one of the postcards to him.

The chief had never seen a picture of himself before. When he returned home, he presented the postcard to Olga. She took a dab of sticky pitch and stuck the postcard on the log wall of their cabin, next to the front window. All winter it would remind her of the grizzly at squirrel camp, the stranded beluga below the berry slopes, long rows of stretchers, tired hands, and sore fingers. The postcard also brought Olga great pride and satisfaction. She knew that the parky, which had taken a year to make, was now multiplied into thick bundles of postcards. She knew it would be seen by people in many other villages and towns. Nothing like this had ever happened in Knik before.

As she looked at the postcard, the heavy log door slammed shut all by itself. A cold breeze ran across Olga's bare feet, and she reached down to massage her toes. Winter was coming. The season of bare feet was past. Mukluks and mittens needed sewing. Hoods needed mending. The bundles of dried salmon in the cache must be turned so they would not spoil. More wood should be chopped, and kindling gathered.

Olga had finished Chief Stephen's parky just in time.

About the Characters and Places

Although the Athapascan Indians are an important Native American linguistic group, little popular literature about them exists. This book attempts to fill in that gap a bit, to show some of the major aspects of the seasonal round that was traditional in the Cook Inlet area of Alaska before the white man came.

Although this book is historical fiction, it is based on records of how the Tanaina, the Athapascans of Upper Cook Inlet, lived a century ago. However, the actual occurrences are the products of imagination.

Olga, Gronia, John, and most of the characters of the book are invented. However, Chief Stephen, Red Shirt, and Orville Herning were real people.

Chief Stephen

Chief Stephen or "Big Stephen" was a tall man, and an important leader. He was about twenty-five years old in 1898. He had a brother named Ruf Stephen. Ruf died in 1948 at over 70 years of age. Ruf had eleven sons and daughters, one of whom, Alice, married Bailey Theodore (1912–1984). Alice and Bailey lived at Knik and had twenty-one children. Many descendants of this family still live in Alaska. Some of them were interviewed for

*Athapascan Chief Stephen stands on the front porch of
Orville Herning's store in the early 1900s. His parky is made
of ground squirrel skins with the tails attached. His necklace
is made of tusk-shaped dentalium shells and beads, spaced
with pieces of caribou or moose hide.*

this book. Many of them still go to summer fish camp
every year.

Two photos of Chief Stephen exist. One, taken by
Orville Herning, appears above; a copy is in the collection of the author.

The other appears in *Shem Pete's Alaska.* It shows
Stephen at a fish camp on Ship Creek, in what is now
the railroad yard and warehouse section of the city of
Anchorage. Stephen is suitably dressed for the rugged
work of fish camp in a shirt and trousers. A woman and
child appear in the photo with him.

Foreign Explorers

For many centuries, Northern Athapascans lived a life that was little affected by occurrences outside their hunting territory. Gradually, however, Russian trappers, English explorers and American soldiers and prospectors entered the country and began to change the traditional way of life in Cook Inlet and elsewhere in Alaska.

By the year 1898 when this story takes place, important changes had already begun to occur in the lives of the Tanaina or *Dena'ina*. In 1741, the Russian Tsarina, Caterina, sent the great Danish explorer, Vitus Bering, across the Bering Sea from Kamchatka to claim whatever land he found. Bering found Alaska. When the survivors of the expedition returned to Russia, they had nine

Sixteen years after the story of Olga and her parky took place, Anchorage began as a tent city.

hundred valuable sea otter pelts with them, and the beauty of these pelts inspired Russian hunters and trappers to begin exploring the new land. They probably made their way to Knik by 1835.

Word of the fur trade soon reached other countries. France and England were hungry for furs, too. Captain James Cook of England came sailing into the Knik Arm of Cook's Inlet in the summer of 1778, looking for a northwest passage. Between May 26th and June 6th, Cook's two ships explored and mapped the inlet. On May 30th, two kayak-style canoes approached them, coming from the Kustatan or Tyonek areas on the west shore, but Cook's ships did not land there. On May 31st, near North Foreland or Tyonek, a group of men, women and children sailed out to Cook's ships in a large *umiak* and several small kayaks, displaying a summer tunic as a sign of friendship. They boarded the ships. Cook also explored Knik Arm.

The Gold Rush

In 1867, the U.S. bought Alaska from Russia. The big, cold country, called "Seward's Icebox," was now an American territory. When gold was discovered in the Yukon Territory of Canada, Americans began looking for alternate routes to the Klondike—and new places to stake out claims. In 1888, Charles Miller discovered gold on Resurrection Creek, at the south end of Cook Inlet. This brought an 1896 stampede of 3,000 prospectors to the Kenai Peninsula, many of them landing at Tyonek, where there was a trading post. Some went north past Knik to the Susitna River and headed inland to search for gold.

The year 1898 was a year of transition for Chief Stephen's family and the other Athapascans of the area. Thousands of prospectors were coming to Cook Inlet. Many were settling at Hope, Sunrise, and Knik. They anchored their big ships at Knik Anchorage on Ship Creek (a site today called Anchorage) to unload supplies, then brought supplies by barge or smaller boats to Tyonek and Knik. They built trails into the interior. They competed with the Indians for game, lumber and firewood.

The Tanaina were beginning to own guns, to trade with the outsiders, to serve as their guides up remote rivers, to speak new words, eat new foods and wear cloth garments. They were beginning to drink China tea and use steel needles. Since missionaries had been assigned to the Cook Inlet area in 1841, many Tanaina had become members of the Russian Orthodox Church. Stephen was named for a Russian saint when he was baptized on one of the visits of the Kenai priest.

Trade and New Trails

Other chiefs in the area at this time were Evan Nicholai, Nikita, Chief Pete of Tyonek, Affinassa, Chief Tyoon, Old Wasilla and John Evan (Simeon Esi). Several of the Tanaina men owned boats and carried freight and government mail. They also earned cash by cutting mine timbers and firewood and by catching and selling fish. Fish were caught in basket traps and with weirs and dip nets. The dried salmon were stored in caches near their winter villages. Indian women sewed beautiful parkys, summer caribou skin tunics, warm moccasins and mittens for trade, and picked barrels of wild cranberries for shipment to Seattle.

The Alaska Commercial Company had a trading post

These buildings show the Russian Orthodox influence in Alaska in the 1800s. Olga's Russian name is part of the same influence.

at Knik at this time. In 1898 ACC issued an advertising booklet to attract more whites to the area. It spoke of the "balmy climate" of Cook Inlet and mentioned the wealth that might be found through "hydraulic mining" of gold.

The U.S. Government was trying to find new routes to the Klondike. Captain Edward F. Glenn, commander of the 25th U.S. Infantry, came to the area to blaze new trails. In 1899, he estimated the Tanaina population around Knik at 149.

Orville Herning

In 1898 Orville G. Herning (1868–1947) was thirty years old. Like many Americans, he was excited about tales of gold strikes in the Far North. He was chosen as leader of Expedition No. 4 of the Klondike Boston Company, a prospecting expedition sponsored by a Boston, Massachusetts, brokerage company. There were ten men in the group. With a heavy camera and fragile glass plates as part of his baggage, Herning landed on the beach at Tyonek south of Knik.

Herning found little gold. To earn a living, he opened a store in his small log house in Knik. He called it Knik Trading Company, Outfitters. Here he lived with his

Orville Herning and a prospecting party with an Indian guide (front) at Susitna Station trading post in 1898. He has marked his position in his own hand.

wife and two sons, close to Knik Arm and Chief Stephen's house. The settlers' houses of Knik were all very
similar—spruce logs, with whipsawn furniture, wood
stoves and chimneys of local blue clay. Although Herning was now a store keeper, he still felt the lure of prospecting. He did some mining in the Willow Creek area
of which Hatcher Pass is part. He filed dozens of claims
and by 1904 was using hydraulic equipment at the Pass.
He continued to take photos until his death. Most of his
photos are now in the collection of the Elmer Rasmuson
Library at the University of Alaska, Fairbanks.

Klondike Boston changed the landscape of Knik forever by building two rough wagon trails out of the village for the purpose of transporting gold mining
equipment. Olga and Gronia followed one of these trails
to ground squirrel camp.

There were more changes to come for the Knik vil-

*Knik, Alaska was a white settlement on the water.
Athapascans also lived there. Orville Herning's store is in the
center with the open door.*

lages. One was the famous Iditarod Trail, built for carrying freight north from Knik during the winter. Freight was unloaded at Ship Creek from big sailing ships and lightered on smaller ships to Knik. The Iditarod, which utilized frozen rivers in order to avoid cutting trails along their banks, was fully established soon after the Innoko-Iditarod gold strike of 1909. The trail, now stretching 1,100 miles to Nome, was re-opened for an annual sled dog race in 1967.

When the route of the Alaska Railroad was laid out, it bypassed Sunny Knik. Herning decided to move his business a few miles north to Wasilla, to be closer to the railroad line. He built a bigger, frame store at Wasilla in about 1916. He called it Herning's Place or K.T. Company. In 1947 the store was sold to Walter and Vivian Teeland, who called it Teeland's. Until 1988, when the building was moved to make way for a new filling station, Teeland's, with its ancient cash register, was a local landmark. It is listed on the National Register of Historic Sites.

Hatcher Pass

Hatcher Pass, where Olga and Gronia snared ground squirrels, is still inhabited by ground squirrels and marmots. Over 60,000 visitors come here between July 4 and Labor Day every year, to view the old mine buildings and admire Lynx Peak and the abundant wildflowers. Winter visitors enjoy skiing and snowmobiling.

Red Shirt Lake

Red Shirt Lake is part of the Nancy Lake State Recreation Area. It is one of the few Alaskan state parks that has been preserved in its natural state as a flat, lake-studded area for recreation. The giant glaciers, which once filled the Susitna River Valley, left thousands of small lakes when they retreated. This particular area is used for canoeing, fishing and boating in a network of more than 130 lakes and ponds. The glacial history of the area shows that the Lower Susitna Valley was clear of ice about 9,000 years ago, allowing for early occupation by man. Archeologists believe the area was heavily used by Tanaina and possibly by Pacific Eskimos. In other words, Chief Stephen's people could have been coming here for muskrat camp and ice fishing for centuries.

Red Shirt

Red Shirt was a rich man who lived at Tanltunt (Red Shirt Lake) part of the year. His Tanaina name was *K'el Nuts'ehen*. He was second chief, or *yagashchik*, of Susitna Station. He caught trout at Red Shirt Lake and sold them at Susitna Station. He was generous with his cloth and bread, and loved to feed children and tell them stories. He died about 1916 and is buried at the lake that bears his name.

One photo of Red Shirt exists. It can be found in the Smithsonian *Handbook of American Indians*, in the section on Athapascans.

The Beluga Whale

The belukha or beluga (*Delphinapterus leucas*) is a medium-sized cetacean belonging to the group known as toothed whales or odontocetes, a group that includes

Orville Herning typed the title on this photograph: "Happy Days on the Susitna 1898." This is a summer fish camp. The women at the left are holding babies in birch bark cradles.

sperm whales, killer whales, dolphins, and porpoises. Its closest relative is the narwhal. Belugas are also called white whales, but they do not actually turn white until they are older. Belugas can live up to forty years.

At birth beluga whales are dark blue-gray in color. They are about five feet long and weigh 90 to 130 pounds. Their color gradually lightens, and they are usually creamy white by age five or six. Adult males are eleven to fifteen feet long and weigh one to two thousand pounds.

Belugas eat herring, capelin, smelt, arctic and saffron cod, salmon and, sculpin. Most of their feeding is done over the continental shelf and in estuaries and river mouths.

This whale occurs throughout arctic and subarctic waters of North America, Greenland, Europe, and Asia. In Alaska, they live in Cook Inlet and the Shelikof Straits and range throughout the Bering, Chukchi, and Beaufort seas. Occasionally they swim up large rivers such as the Yukon.

Belugas are very vocal mammals, producing a variety of grunts, clicks, chirps, and whistles, which they use for navigating, finding prey, and communicating with one another. Their nickname is sea canary.

The Cook Inlet population of belugas is estimated at four to five hundred. The Tanaina used them as a source of *muktuk*, a food that consists of the skin and outer layer of blubber. Their oil was used for cooking and for fuel. Whale oil was also used to rub down human babies.

Notes

The names of John's dogs, Sodaa and Kanaa, are based on Koyukon Athapascan words. Sodaa is used when addressing an older sister. Kanaa means something like "good speaker," and is meant to indicate that this dog has quite a voice.

The ground squirrel story that Olga tells Gronia at Hatcher Pass is adapted from the story *"Ounsha Sukdu'a"* told by Antone Evan (born about 1920 at a village on the Upper Stony River). The story appears in a book compiled by Joan Tenenbaum of Anchorage, *Dena'ina Sukdu'a: Traditional Stories of the Tanaina Athapaskans,* published in 1984 by the Alaska Native Language Center in Fairbanks. The story is one of the Dghiliq' Sukdu'a or "mountain stories" in the collection. Many of these stories teach lessons about how game will disappear if men and women do not follow strict hunting protocol.

The berry pudding is adapted from *Dena'ina T'qit'-ach' (The Way the Tanainas Are),* published by the Alaska Native Language Center in 1975. This is a collection of brief recollections and stories by living Tanaina informants. Some details of beluga processing and fish smoking are also derived from this source.

About the Author

Ann Chandonnet has lived in Alaska for twenty years. While living near the village of Eklunta, she became intrigued with the local native American culture and began to research it, taking ten years to study the Athapascans of Cook Inlet. Ann is currently involved in a museum exhibit called "Shadows" at the International Gallery of Art in Anchorage. Her poem, "Words for Shadows," is part of the background music for artist Peter Bevis's bronze sculptures, which are cast from the remains of the sea otters who perished in the Exxon Valdez oil spill in 1989. The exhibit is designed to remind people to care for our natural world.

If you liked *Chief Stephen's Parky,* you'll like other books in The Council for Indian Education Series. Roberts Rinehart publishes books for all ages, both fiction and non-fiction, in the subjects of natural and cultural history. For more information about all of our books, please write or call for a catalog.

Roberts Rinehart
P.O. Box 666
Niwot, CO 80544

1-800-352-1985